Rachel Isadora
In the Beginning

G. P. Putnam's Sons
in association with Funny Face Books

In the
beginning
there was
only heaven
and earth.

Then . . .

light

sky

land and sea

every kind of plant

sun

moon and stars

creatures of the
sea and
sky

creatures
of the land

Love

and then

you